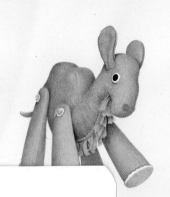

Little Bear's
Trousers

For my mother – in her memory

Library of Congress Cataloging-in-Publication Data
Hissey, Jane.   Little Bear's Trousers.
Summary: While looking for his missing trousers,
Little Bear discovers that other animals have found many
different uses for them.
[1. Bears—Fiction. 2. Trousers—Fiction] I.   Title
PZ7.H627Li 1987 [E] 87-7806
ISBN 0-399-21493-3

First impression

JANE HISSEY

Little Bear's Trousers

Philomel Books
New York

THE sun shone through the window and woke
Little Bear. "What a lovely morning," he said
to himself. "I'll do something different today."

HE jumped down from the bed, took off his pajamas and looked for his trousers.

He looked on the chair where he'd left them and he looked on the floor under the chair – and then he looked through the chest of drawers in case they were there. But they weren't. They were nowhere.

"But they must be somewhere," said Little Bear. "Trousers don't disappear. I'll go and ask Old Bear. *He'll* know where they are."

OLD Bear was already enjoying the sun in his deckchair. "I haven't seen your trousers, I'm afraid," he said. "But Camel was around here earlier. Perhaps she knows where they are."

"OH dear," said Camel, when Little Bear found her a few minutes later. "I did find them. I thought they were a pair of hump warmers and I tried them on to see if they fitted me. They did keep my humps *quite* warm but the air came down the tops so I decided these were better." And she showed Little Bear two very smart pom-pom hats – one for each hump.

"I gave the old hump warmers to Sailor to use as sails for his boat. Jump on my back and let's see if we can find him." Little Bear scrambled up and they galloped off in the direction of the bathroom.

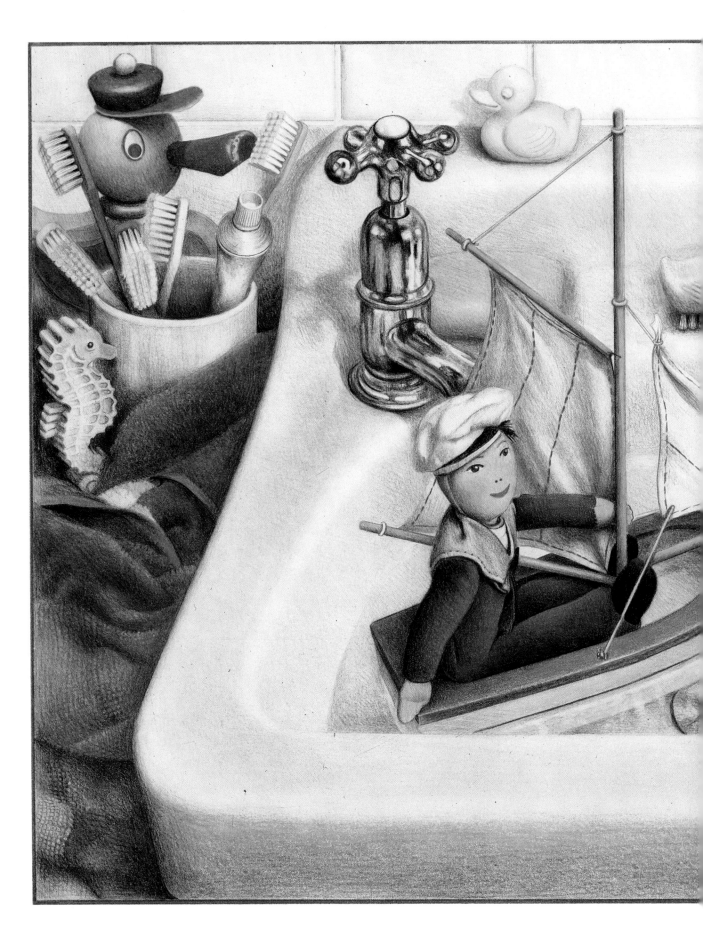

SAILOR was looking after the boats and ducks in the bathroom. "I did use them as sails," he said, "but they looked too much like trousers."

"That's because they *are* trousers," said Little Bear crossly. "Where are they now?"

"I gave them to Dog to keep his bones in," said Sailor. "Sorry, Little Bear. We'd better hurry, he might be anywhere by now."

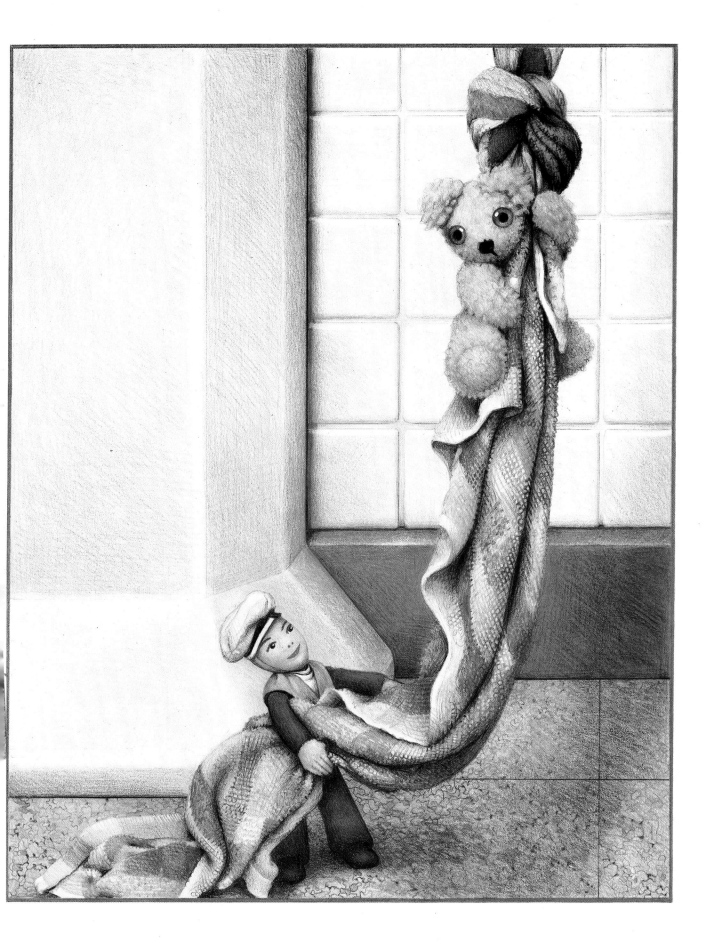

DOG was happily burying his bones in flowerpots when Little Bear found him. "My bones kept falling through the two-bone bone-holder," he said.

"TWO-BONE BONE-HOLDER!" cried Little Bear in dismay. "Oh, Dog, can't you recognize trousers when you see them?"

"Oh, dear," said Dog. "I do feel silly. I gave them to Rabbit – he said he needed a skiing hat, and your trousers looked just perfect. I am sorry."

"WHEEE!" cried Rabbit, as he shot past Little Bear a few minutes later, skiing down the bannister on two lollipop stick skis. He didn't have Little Bear's trousers on his head now.

"But I did have them earlier," he explained when Little Bear caught up with him. "They made a lovely rabbit hat, with plenty of room for my ears. But they slipped over my eyes and I crashed, so I decided it was safer without them. I gave them to Zebra to carry her building bricks in."

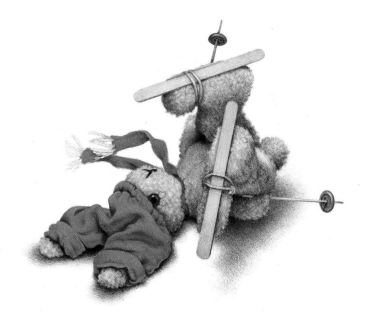

ZEBRA was building herself a house when Little Bear arrived. But his trousers were nowhere to be seen.

"I wondered whose they were," she said. "They were terribly useful. I tied up the legs with string, put them on my back and carried all these bricks here in them. But when I had enough bricks for my house I gave them to Duck to use as a flag for his sand castle. I am sorry, Little Bear. I didn't know they belonged to you."

DUCK was in the sand tray looking sadly at the castle he'd made. There was no trouser flag on the top now. "I did use the flag that Zebra gave me," he sighed. "But Bramwell Brown came and said it was just what he needed, urgently, in the kitchen. He gave me this paper flag to use instead."

"Never mind," said Little Bear with a sigh, feeling quite glad that his trousers were not covered in sand.

The kitchen was in a terrible muddle. There were bowls and spoons and eggs and flour, and in the middle of it all sat Bramwell Brown.

HE had Little Bear's trousers but, oh dear, he'd filled them with pink icing and was busy decorating a huge cake with them.

"It's a special occasion cake," said Bramwell. "And you have to put icing on special occasion cakes. I thought I could do two stripes at once with these icing bags."

"But they're *not* icing bags. They are my trousers!" sniffed Little Bear, trying hard not to cry.

"I thought I'd seen them before," said Bramwell Brown.

"DON'T worry, Little Bear," said Old Bear, who always arrived at the right moment. "The icing will wash out and they'll look as good as new."

"What's the special occasion cake for?" asked Little Bear, feeling a bit more cheerful at this news.

"Well, I didn't really know," said Bramwell. "I just felt like making one."

Old Bear thought hard. "Perhaps it ought to be a Trousers Day Cake," he suggested helpfully.

So that's what Bramwell Brown wrote on the cake. Twice. Once with the icing from the left trouser leg and once with the icing from the right trouser leg. It said Happy Trousers Day in the middle, and there was a trousers pattern all round the edge.

DUCK washed Little Bear's trousers and dried them next to the stove. Then all the toys sat down to enjoy a piece of cake and to celebrate the day Little Bear lost, and found, his trousers.

AND ever since Trousers Day, Little Bear has slept with his trousers under his pillow. "Nobody will find them there," he says.